# The Secret Dinosaur
# Book 3
## *Jurassic Adventure*

## N.S.Blackman

**db**

Dinosaur Books

Text and illustrations copyright © 2014, 2015
N.S.Blackman

All Rights Reserved
Published by Dinosaur Books Ltd, London
This edition: 2015
www.dinosaurbooks.co.uk
Dinoteks™ Sonya McGilchrist

The right of N.S.Blackman to be identified as the
author and illustrator of this work has been
asserted by him in accordance with the
Copyright, Designs and Patents Act, 1988

ISBN 978-0-9927525-2-1
British Library Cataloguing in Publication Data
A CIP catalogue record for this book is available from
the British Library

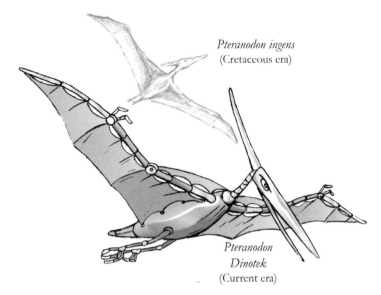

*Pteranodon ingens*
(Cretaceous era)

*Pteranodon Dinotek*
(Current era)

# The Secret Dinosaur - 3

## By N.S.Blackman

*Centrosaurus*
(Cretaceous era)

*Centrosaurus Dinotek*
(Current era)

Also available in the **Dinoteks** series

*The Secret Dinosaur Book 1*
*The Secret Dinosaur Book 2*
*The Secret Dinosaur Book 4*
*The Lost Dinosaur* (for younger readers)

Visit www.dinoteks.com for the latest titles,
puzzles and activities featuring the Dinoteks!
visit www.dinoteks.com for the latest titles

# About the Dinoteks

Next time you go to a museum look out for the dusty old dinosaur that nobody else is interested in.

There's usually one.

Most people think it's just an old museum statue, left over from the days when models weren't very realistic.

But if you know what to look for, and if you are really lucky, you might discover an amazing secret.

Dinoteks are more than statues or models or even dinosaurs.

Dinoteks are living machines.

**www.dinoteks.com**

For all dinosaur friends
wherever you are
- remember the Three Golden Rules!

# The Story So Far

......................

## How the Dinoteks escaped

It took them four days and nights but they did it. The Dinoteks escaped from their enemies and came safely to the Jurassic Mountain.

This is what happened next…

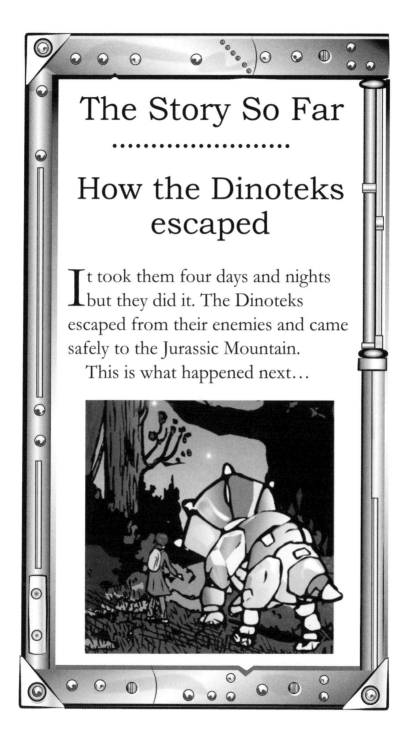

# Chapter One

## Plunging In

Marlin Maxton was just an ordinary boy until he reached the age of ten. And then, when he was exactly ten years and two months old, he became the luckiest boy ever.

Can you imagine having a full-size T-Rex for a friend? And escaping with a family of dinosaurs on a train in the middle of the night? And going to live with them on a mountain?

Well Marlin Maxton was even luckier than that.

Marlin's friends were *Dinoteks*, living dinosaur machines – which meant they could think and talk and fly and run incredibly fast. And they also had all sorts of amazing powers.

Which was lucky, because right now Marlin really needed help…

*******

He was clutching onto the root of a tree as he dangled over the edge of a steep bank with his feet in a river. The cold water was filling his trainers, soaking up his trouser legs. He looked down again and felt a lurch of fear. The river was flowing fast and deep.

"Help!" he shouted. "Flame! Quick!"

There was no reply.

Marlin was carrying a heavy rucksack and that made it hard for him to move and hard to hang on. His fingers slipped on the muddy tree root.

He thought fast (as people do when they find themselves in immediate danger).

One: the bag was heavy. If he was still wearing it when he fell into water he would sink like a stone.

Two: he couldn't just drop the bag because inside it were many precious things that he'd spent a long time collecting. And, even more importantly, in the bag was also the one thing that the Dinoteks needed to survive: the golden power-charger that restored their batteries and gave them energy. If that went into the river it might never work again.

And three…

But before he got to three his fingers slipped again and he heard himself crying out.

"Help!"

*******

Marlin had spent a whole week living on the mountain, being very adventurous and resourceful. He'd even begun to think of himself as someone quite brave. But now his voice sounded different. It came out like a frightened squeak.

"I'm falling!"

And then, just in time, he saw it…

A broken root sticking out of the bank just below him.

*Use it as a hook! Hang the bag there…*

    With the last
of his strength
Marlin managed
to get the precious bag
onto the sticking-out-root.

  And a second later he fell.

   Marlin fell and just before the cold
water engulfed him  another thought raced
through his mind. Why had he called Flame

anyway? The Dinotek T-Rex couldn't help him. Flame was a machine powered by electricity – one splash of water on his computer circuits and he'd probably be destroyed.

With this final thought he plunged into the water and freezing darkness engulfed him and took away his breath.

Then, almost immediately, he felt himself being lifted up again and dropped onto the river bank.

He coughed, shook the water from his eyes – and gasped. There was Flame, standing below him in the river! The icy water swirled around the T-Rex's legs and splashed all over his metal body.

"Get out…" panted Marlin. "Flame, quick! Your circuits will be soaked!"

The creature shrugged.

"I'm fine."

Marlin sat up and stared at him.

"Really, I'm fine," said Flame.

Marlin was astonished.

"Flame, you're waterproof!" he laughed.

"Yes," replied the T-Rex.

N.S.Blackman

"But how did you know?"

Flame grinned.

"I didn't."

*******

"What are you doing in there?!" snapped a voice.

It was Steg. The Dinotek had appeared among the trees behind Marlin. His armour plates rattled crossly.

"You'll go rusty you silly Rex! Get out!"

"I'm waterproof," grunted Flame.

The T-Rex took two strides and climbed up the bank, bringing Marlin's back-pack with him. The water cascaded off his metal body and splashed into the undergrowth.

"That was easy. I might learn to swim next," he grinned.

"You'd just sink," snorted the Stegosaur.

Marlin laughed.

"What are you doing Steg?"

"Looking out for enemies of course," the Dinotek replied. "Somebody has to keep watch…"

And he turned, with a swipe of his spiked tail, and stomped off into the trees.

*******

"We've been here a whole week," grunted Flame. "Why doesn't he relax?"

Marlin shrugged – then he shivered.

He was soaked through.

"Hold up your arms," said the T-Rex.

Marlin lifted them and Flame took a deep

breath – and blew.

Marlin shut his eyes and let the warm air rush over him. It was like standing in front of a massive fan. Flame's mechanical lungs were big and the air kept blowing and blowing until Marlin's face and hair and clothes were totally dry. He pulled off his soaking trainers and held them up too.

"More!"

Flame took another deep breath – and blew so hard that Marlin fell over!

"You did that on purpose!"

Marlin lobbed one of the trainers – CLANG! It was a good shot and it bounced off Flame's nose.

That made them both laugh – and if you've never seen a T-Rex laugh you won't know that sometimes they roll over and kick their legs in the air (but only if it's really funny).

Marlin sighed and sat up.

"We'd better get back to the others."

Flame stood.

"You're right, they'll be waiting!"

And then Flame took hold of Marlin in his teeth and threw him up into the air. The boy somersaulted and landed perfectly on top of the great creature.

They'd been practising this move all week – and by now they were so good at it that Marlin could actually land right in the special seat on Flame's back.

"Let's go!"

# Chapter Two

•••••••••••••••

## On the
## Jurassic Mountain

The Dinoteks were gathered around the cave that Protos had made his home. Marlin took off his back-pack and they all waited while Protos rummaged around inside the cave.

Since they had arrived on the mountain each of them had found a special place to live.

Dacky had settled on a very tall fir tree. When he perched near the top he could see for miles. Steg had found an old building. It was ruined and collapsed, with no roof and no doors, but that was OK because it made it easy for him to get in and out. Flame had found a hollow on the mountainside, covered with pine trees. The trees weren't too close together, so he could move about, but they were still dense and dark enough for him to feel snug.

Little Dragon liked flitting up and down the river during the day and

each night he settled down on a smooth boulder.

The Troodons couldn't decide where to live. They'd spent a whole day scampering about trying to choose. So instead of having their own home, each night they went between Steg and Flame – and sometimes back again.

And Protos had the cave.

N.S.Blackman

It wasn't what a real Centrosaurus would have chosen in the Cretaceous era, he explained – caves were more suitable for bears. But it reminded him of the museum.

He had made it very comfortable and Marlin had even borrowed some planks from Steg's ruined house and helped him to make some shelves.

Protos already had three books on

them and a collection of fossils.

Where did he get the books from?

It happened like this...

Marlin had worked out a way for them to get supplies.

On their journey to the Jurassic Mountain they had passed a village with a small shop in it. It was one of those useful country shops that sells everything.

Now they didn't have any money, but they did have something that might be valuable. This was Marlin's idea.

The Dinoteks gathered around and he opened his back-pack. He tipped out all the things he'd been collecting.

Fossils! There were lots of them on the mountain – curling shapes, leafy shapes, spiky shapes, beautiful bones and claws, all set in stone, frozen in time.

"Excellent," said Protos.

Then the old creature went into his cave and came back out holding a piece of paper. He'd spent a long time working on it and it was covered in neat writing – very large letters, but carefully done.

Marlin read it out to everyone.

DEAR SIR OR MADAM, HERE ARE SOME VALUABLE FOSSILS THAT VISITORS TO YOUR SHOP MIGHT LIKE TO BUY. IF YOU HAVE SOME FOOD THAT I COULD TAKE IN EXCHANGE I WOULD BE VERY GRATEFUL. WE'D LIKE SOME SANDWICHES. AND CHOCOLATE IS GOOD, BUT NOT MINTS. ALSO, DO YOU HAVE ANY BOOKS? AND IF POSSIBLE, A CAN OF MACHINE OIL.

THANK YOU.

Dacky nodded.

"One of my wings squeaked this

morning. I need oil."

Dacky took the note in his beak, scooped the fossils up and took off into the sky.

The plan was simple. Dacky would wait outside the village until night, then when it got dark he would fly in and leave the note outside the shop underneath the pile of fossils.

When he went back the next night (they hoped) there would be a bag left outside with all their supplies in it.

\*\*\*\*\*\*\*

It worked. So the morning after Marlin had a nice meal and some chocolate. He went to each of the Dinoteks dripping oil onto their joints.

He powered-up their batteries too, using Uncle Gus's golden power-charger.

Even Steg cheered up.

After that, each time they needed supplies, Dacky would take a note and some fossils to the shop.

So Marlin knew he really was the luckiest boy in the world – and that this was the best way to spend the school holidays.

*******

After several days, Protos made an announcement.

"I'm having a special party tonight. It's to celebrate our first week here. Will everyone come?"

They all cheered.

"Yes of course," grunted Steg. "Straight after my evening patrol I'll join you."

Protos smiled – but even so Marlin thought that he looked a bit sad.

# Chapter Three

• • • • • • • • • • • • •

## Around the Camp Fire

Everyone spent the whole day getting ready.

Protos gathered up rocks and laid them out in a circle in front of his cave. The Troodons brought twigs and sticks and piled them up inside the circle, arranging them very carefully. Then Dacky arranged them again, a bit differently, and put some thicker branches on top.

They were going to have a camp fire.

Marlin and Flame planned a special surprise. Marlin climbed high up into a tree (with a lift-up from Flame) and began tying a rope between the branches.

The ground was a long way below but he wasn't scared.

When he looked down he saw that Protos was talking to Flame – and when the T-Rex looked back up at him Marlin thought he looked troubled.

"What's wrong?" Marlin asked him, after Protos had gone again.

"Oh, nothing," he answered. "Protos is worried you'll get hurt…"

Marlin laughed.

"Well I'm fine with you here! Come on Flame – let's get this finished…"

"Yes," nodded the T-Rex. "Let's go and find the leaves."

Then they raced down the stony track that led through the forest, down the mountain.

Down here the trees were different. They weren't tall pine trees and firs, but oaks and ashes with broad leaves.

Perfect for what they wanted.

******

The party began as soon as the sun went down.

Protos lit the fire and sparks went crackling up into the gloom like orange fireworks.

Marlin sat on a large, smooth boulder. Flame had found it in the river. It was shaped a bit like a chair (or as near to that shape as a boulder ever gets) and it wasn't wet because it had spent the whole day in the sun warming up.

The Dinoteks gathered around and the firelight sparkled on their metal faces.

The party began with Protos giving an 'interesting talk'. This was about an important new fossil he had found. It was a footprint fossil, possibly from a juvenile sauropod.

Then Dacky told everyone his news. He spread his great wings and announced that he was planning to fly right over the top of the mountain.

"It will be a very risky adventure and it will take all my skill and experience," he said gravely. "But I think I can do it."

Little Dragon began buzzing around frantically but nobody could quite understand what he was saying.

"I think he wants to go with you… to make sure you're OK," whispered Protos to Dacky.

"Oh, I see," nodded Dacky. Then he cleared his throat:

"Ahem! Anyone who can fly is also welcome to come to the top of the mountain."

Little Dragon buzzed happily and landed on the ground right next to the Pterosaur.

Then Steg arrived from his evening patrol and they all shuffled round to make room for him. Protos thought it would only be fair on Steg if he started his 'interesting talk' again, right at the beginning – so he did. And this time he also added some useful information about sauropod migration patterns.

Then the Troodons jumped up and asked for a story.

"Professor Marlin! Tell us about the Bad Machine!"

"He's not a professor," snorted Steg.

"Tell us! Tell us!"

The Dinoteks all turned to Marlin.

So he stood up and told the story of how the hunter's helicopter had tried to catch them on their escape to the mountain.

(The helicopter was totally black and it belonged to Snickenbacker – which Marlin had guessed. Snickenbacker called it the Raptor – which Marlin couldn't have guessed, but wouldn't have been surprised by).

"Three times the hunters flew over the amazing Dinoteks in their black helicopter, and three times the amazing Dinoteks heard it coming and quickly hid," said Marlin, telling his story.

"Protos hid by a hedge. Steg hid in a bush. Flame hid under a tree. And everyone else hid under Flame. And so the amazing Dinoteks got safely to Jurassic Mountain, which belongs to them…"

They cheered.

"And now…" he announced, "Flame and I have a surprise for you all!"

Flame stood up.

He stretched his golden head up into the trees and shook the branches. A cloud of leaves came tumbling and fluttering down all about them – and there, hanging high in the tree, was a large sheet of wood with letters drawn on it in black and white.

Marlin had written the letters using white chalk (from the ground) and black charcoal (from burnt wood).

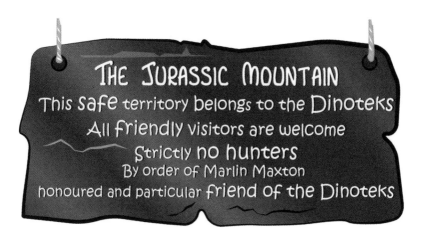

**THE JURASSIC MOUNTAIN**
This safe territory belongs to the Dinoteks
All friendly visitors are welcome
Strictly no hunters
By order of Marlin Maxton
honoured and particular friend of the Dinoteks

Protos read it out loud to everyone and they cheered again – and now even Steg was impressed.

"That's good. That's very good. We should put it at the bottom of the mountain," he said, "To mark the edge of our land."

"Flame told me to write the last line," shrugged Marlin modestly.

And then Protos stood up.

"The last line is very true," said the old creature. "Marlin Maxton, you are our honoured and particular friend."

"What does honodanticular mean?" squeaked Comp.

"It means best friend," hissed Dacky.

And as Marlin sat back on his warm, comfortable chair, he felt as happy as he could ever imagine feeling. There was no doubt about it, he was the luckiest boy on the planet.

# Chapter Four

........................

## Things a Boy Must Do

When Marlin woke next morning he was at home, in bed.

*No!*

He sat up.

*I can't be … what…what happened?!*

His room looked exactly as he'd left it a whole week ago. Nothing had changed.

*The mountain…the Dinoteks… Protos…how can I be back here?…*

The door opened and his mum came in. Her arms were piled so high with clothes that her chin was resting on the top. She began stuffing jumpers, t-shirts and socks into his wardrobe.

"Hello dear," she said cheerfully. "You were out late. Is everything OK?"

"Yes but I…"

"Oh good. What have you been doing?"

"Mum I shouldn't be here! I was…"

"Really? That's nice!"

Then she came over and sat on his bed.

"I'm sorry we've been so busy lately. Dad and I have got just one more business trip to do, that's all. Then we can have a few days together with you. If you like we can go and see a film, or something?"

"That would be great Mum but…"

She gave him a hug – and then she was gone again.

Marlin scrambled out of bed.

Having busy parents was good and bad. It meant he could do most things he wanted without asking. But it also meant that sometimes there was nobody to talk to.

"OK," he said to himself. "First things first. Was it all a dream? Please don't let it be that…"

But no – his clothes – he was still wearing

the old leather jacket from the museum. His trousers were covered in mud and his skin smelled of wood-smoke.

"So I definitely wasn't dreaming – but why am I back here?…"

He ran to the window. There was a line of massive three-toed footprints on the lawn – one trail coming towards his window and another leading away again. And they were fresh prints because the grass was still squashed down – and it wouldn't take long for it to spring up and be growing straight again.

"So it was Flame. He must have run all the way from the mountain and carried me back here last night. But why?…"

"Goodbye love!" his Mum called up the stairs. "See you tonight!"

BANG!

The front door slammed shut.

Marlin stood there for a moment rubbing the sleep out of his eyes.

He had a lot to do and he was already making a list in his head.

The first things were: 1) shower 2) clean

clothes 3) breakfast and 4) find Uncle Gus.

On second thoughts he decided to skip straight to number four.

*******

Uncle Gus was working on the strangest-looking machine that Marlin had ever seen.

It was as big as a wardrobe, made of wood, and had a glass front and a confusion of brass fittings – handles, knobs and levers.

Uncle Gus was busy connecting wires.

His face lit up as soon as he saw Marlin.

"You're back!" he exclaimed.

He dropped the wires and clambered down to give Marlin a hug.

"What happened lad?! Where have you been all week? How are the Dinoteks? No, wait! – first things first – "

And he dashed across the workshop to grab the kettle.

"Tea? Or hot chocolate? Or both?!"

"Hot chocolate," grinned Marlin.

"Good! And we'll have some buttered toast too – we've got a lot to talk about…"

*******

Marlin told Uncle Gus everything that had happened since they'd last been together on the lawn in front of the museum. It felt like such a long time ago.

His uncle leaned forward, listening intently.

"And the Dinoteks? Are they safe?"

"Yes. I mean – I think so. We escaped. And we got to the mountain…"

Then he sighed.

"But I don't understand why Flame brought me home. They didn't say anything Uncle, not even goodbye!"

Uncle Gus nodded thoughtfully.

"They must have had their own reasons lad…"

The old man stared into his cup for a moment then suddenly looked up.

"That's a lovely old coat you're wearing. I used to have one just the same. Very warm I remember. Lots of pockets…"

"Dacky gave it to me. It's from the museum. I shouldn't really have it…"

"Years ago, they were very fashionable," Uncle Gus continued. "Mine used to have a hidden extra pocket for valuable things, just here – "

He pointed to the coat's lining, just behind the lapel.

"Yes, look! You've got one too – a secret zip!"

He was right!

Marlin looked down at the zip and pulled it. A pocket opened. He put his hand inside.

"There's something here ... a piece of paper…"

"Well hurry up, lad! Pull it out and let's have a look!"

The paper seemed quite new – white and crisp, not creased up like the old coat – and it was

neatly folded. Marlin opened it and his heart skipped a beat. His name was written at the top! The paper was covered in writing – large, neat letters.

"What does it say lad?"

Marlin read it out:

TO OUR BEST FRIEND MARLIN,

THIS LETTER IS TO SAY GOODBYE AND TO SAY THANK YOU FOR SAVING US.

WE COULDN'T TELL YOU THAT IT WAS TIME TO GO HOME. WE KNEW THAT YOU WOULDN'T

WANT TO GO AND YOU WOULD PROBABLY ARGUE BECAUSE YOU ARE VERY DETERMINED AND BRAVE.

FLAME IS SAD BUT HE WILL CARRY YOU HOME WHILE YOU ARE SLEEPING.

YOU ARE A BOY — AND THAT MEANS YOU HAVE TO LIVE IN A HOUSE, AND SLEEP IN A BED, AND GO TO SCHOOL AND DO BOY THINGS.

WE HAVE TO LIVE ON THE MOUNTAIN AND DO DINOSAUR THINGS. WE ARE SAFE HERE, AND WE HAVE THE POWER CHARGER, SO DON'T WORRY ABOUT US.

WE WILL NEVER FORGET YOU AND WE WILL THINK ABOUT YOU EVERY DAY.

WITH ALL OUR LOVE

FROM PROTOS, FLAME, STEG, DACKY, COMP, SIGGY AND LITTLE DRAGON.


PS. PLEASE VISIT THE MUSEUM SOMETIMES AND MAKE SURE EVERYTHING IS KEPT NEAT.


Marlin folded up the letter.

It's not fair, that's what he wanted to say – but he knew that saying it wouldn't change anything. He wanted to live on the mountain – but he knew that he couldn't.

He wanted one more week, just one, with the Dinoteks – but he knew he wouldn't get it.

He sighed and hung his head.

Uncle Gus put a hand on his shoulder. "Don't be sad."

He stood and walked over to the window.

"Something tells me your adventure isn't over yet…"

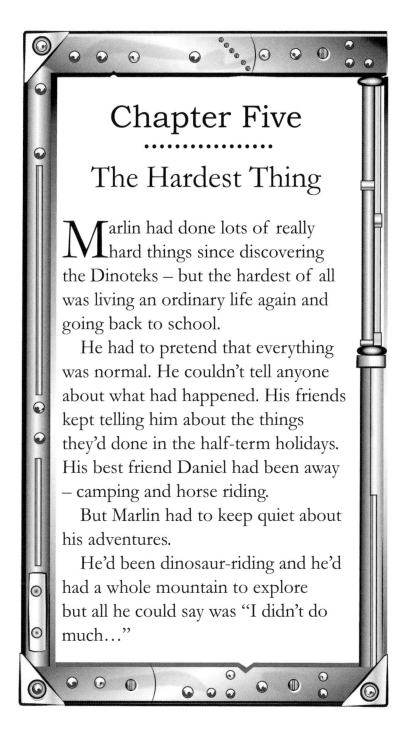

# Chapter Five

·················

## The Hardest Thing

Marlin had done lots of really hard things since discovering the Dinoteks – but the hardest of all was living an ordinary life again and going back to school.

He had to pretend that everything was normal. He couldn't tell anyone about what had happened. His friends kept telling him about the things they'd done in the half-term holidays. His best friend Daniel had been away – camping and horse riding.

But Marlin had to keep quiet about his adventures.

He'd been dinosaur-riding and he'd had a whole mountain to explore but all he could say was "I didn't do much…"

And he couldn't concentrate on his lessons.

On the first morning he got told off twice by Mrs Baxter for staring out of the window. He'd been daydreaming that he was climbing the mountain with Flame.

He sighed.

This was going to be a hard week…

*******

Later that day they had a science lesson about how things fly.

Normally Marlin would have loved that – especially when Mr Morris showed them how to make paper gliders.

"…now I'll just fold the wings a bit

and…"

The glider soared across the room and crashed into the wall.

Everyone cheered. But Marlin couldn't help thinking about Dacky catching the air and soaring upwards…

"I've been flying… I've actually been up there…all the way up…" and his eyes strayed out of the window again and began following a seagull as it swooped across the sky.

"Marlin Maxton, wake up!" exclaimed Mr Morris.

Marlin shook himself awake.

"There's a visitor for you Marlin – you need to go to the school office straight away."

*******

The visitor was Inspector Bailey, the police detective.

She was sitting, reading a notebook when Marlin came in. She glanced up at him with her kind, but keen eyes – and Marlin had the feeling that she could tell, just by looking at him, exactly what he'd been doing.

He had cleaned himself up and scrubbed the smell of wood-smoke out of his hair, but he imagined that she would still be able to tell he'd been lighting camp fires.

"Am I… am I in trouble again?" he began.

"Not with me," she smiled. "I just wanted

to make sure you're OK. Your uncle told me you came home last night – after your trip? He says you've been having an… adventure?"

"Yes…I was away…"

How much could he tell her, Marlin wondered? Did she know about the Dinoteks? And if she did, would she help them?

"I hear you've been exploring in the mountains?"

He nodded.

"And you've been travelling with some – er – friends?"

He nodded again.

Inspector Bailey sighed.

"I've had an interesting week myself…"

She flicked through her notebook and then looked back up at him.

"There are some very odd stories going around – people talking about dinosaurs coming to life. That's what you told me before wasn't it? And I know that Mr Grubbler and his friends have been chasing about in black trucks hunting for mechanical monsters…"

Marlin looked alarmed.

"But it's OK. I think they've given up hunting now," continued the Inspector. "The thing is… if I knew where such creatures might be hiding, and if I thought they were safe there, I probably wouldn't tell anyone about it…"

Marlin looked at her.

She did believe him about the Dinoteks! And she was warning him to keep them secret!

"Are…are the hunters still looking for them?" he asked.

"I don't think so," she replied. "But if the creatures were real it would probably be best if they stayed hidden. Just in case."

She smiled and stood up.

"I can see you've had a good time in the mountains Marlin, you look very healthy!"

And then she shook his hand politely and left.

*******

Marlin tidied up his bedroom and pinned the letter from Protos to the wall next to his bed. It was the most precious thing he now owned.

Each night, before he closed his eyes, he read it again.

*We will never forget you and we will think about you every day…*

He thought about them too.

Every night he dreamed he was back on the mountain.

But when he woke each morning he was disappointed.

*******

Marlin went to see Uncle Gus again. The old man was still working on his strange machine. It got more amazing each time Marlin saw it.

"What is it for, Uncle?"

"I'm still not sure. He grinned. But I'll know when it's finished."

The old man looked up at him.

"Pass me those pliers lad, and you can help me with the wiring…"

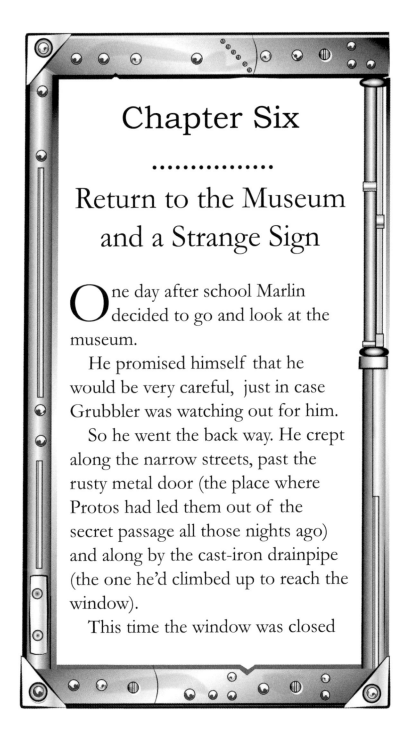

# Chapter Six

. . . . . . . . . . . . . . . .

## Return to the Museum
## and a Strange Sign

One day after school Marlin decided to go and look at the museum.

He promised himself that he would be very careful, just in case Grubbler was watching out for him.

So he went the back way. He crept along the narrow streets, past the rusty metal door (the place where Protos had led them out of the secret passage all those nights ago) and along by the cast-iron drainpipe (the one he'd climbed up to reach the window).

This time the window was closed

and there was no sign of the big security guard.

There was no sign of anyone in fact.

When Marlin reached the end of the road, he heard voices – lots of people all talking at once.

He poked his head around the corner.

*******

Marlin frowned. There was an excited crowd on the lawn in front of the museum. People were tip-toeing to get a better view of something in front of the steps.

*What's going on?...*

He slipped into the crowd. Surely nobody would notice one small boy among all these people?

He squeezed and pushed his way to the front, towards the museum.

*******

The way was blocked. There was a solid wooden fence in front of the museum, covered in signs and posters.

The fence was too high to see over, but everyone was crowding round to read the posters plastered onto it.

Marlin looked at the one nearest to him:

## COMING SOON – A MAJOR NEW ATTRACTION
### The Most Amazing, INCREDIBLE and Fantastic

**Entertainment for the Whole Family!**
**You've never seen anything like it (guaranteed)!**
**Tickets available now from Oliver Grubbler and Howard H. Snickenbacker**

Marlin's first thought was that this was good news. If Grubbler and Snickenbacker were busy with a new scheme then they wouldn't have time to hunt for the Dinoteks.

But what exactly was the new attraction?

He squeezed through the crowd again, going further along the fence. Maybe he could find a way through, and into the museum? He kept low so that nobody would notice him – and that's how he spotted it.

In one of the wooden fence panels, close to the ground, there was a small hole.

*******

Marlin pressed his face up to the hole, squinting to see what was on the other side.

The first thing he saw made his heart lurch. It was the army of black vehicles – the demolition trucks – they were still here!

And there was something else as well. Something strange.

He screwed his eyes up, trying to see…

There, in the middle of all the vehicles, was a weird looking, gigantic machine.

At first it reminded Marlin of a fairground ride, one of those fast ones that spin round and round with arms sticking out on every side.

But no – it wasn't covered in cheerful lights and didn't really look like a ride – what it really looked like was a huge, mechanical spider.

"Is everything ready?" said a voice suddenly, close by.

Marlin froze.

It was Grubbler! Inches away from him, just on the other side of the wooden fence!

"Yes. The Raptor went out again

yesterday and finally found their trail. Now we know where they're hiding…"

"Good. Then the Cruncher will soon have something to fight. And our audience won't be disappointed…"

The Cruncher? *The spider-machine?*

Suddenly an engine revved-up and Marlin couldn't hear any more.

But he'd heard enough.

# Chapter Seven

·················

## The Enemies Meet

Marlin raced to Uncle Gus's workshop, sprinting all the way.

The Dinoteks were in danger – he had to get help!

But this time there was no friendly light shining out from the workshop window. And when he tugged at the door he found it locked.

What now?

Go home? Go back to the museum?

He couldn't think of what to do.

He stumbled back along the overgrown alleyway, feeling small and lost.

Marlin's mind was filled with the thought of that big, ugly machine

– the Cruncher . He imagined it coming to life and attacking his friends. And even before that, they'd be hunted down on the mountain by the Raptor helicopter and the black trucks – and this time their hiding would do no good.

As Marlin thought about all these things he grew angry. And then something strange happened.

As he stumbled along the green path, under the trees and through the long grass, he smelled the sweetness of the air and he had a sudden memory of being back on the mountain.

And I don't know for sure but maybe some magic came over him – the sort of magic that you sometimes find in wild places that makes you feel brave and free.

Marlin wasn't a lost boy any more.

He was an adventurer again.

A feeling of courage rose up inside him. And he'd thought of a plan.

There was one person who might possibly help him right now. Marlin ran to find her.

Most people would have laughed, or not believed him, but Inspector Bailey listened to Marlin very carefully.

"And you think this Cruncher is some sort of fighting machine?"

"Yes! I heard Mr Grubbler talking about it. And the trucks – they're getting them ready again. They're going to catch the Dinoteks and bring them back – to fight!"

"It sounds hard to believe," she said. "Is that what you really think?"

"Yes! I'm sure I'm right," said Marlin.

"I see…"

The Inspector stacked the papers neatly on her desk and stood up.

"Well then, let's go and have a look."

*******

It was starting to get dark. All the people had gone home and the Museum Square was empty. Marlin walked up to the wooden fence with Inspector Bailey.

"They're in here – all the machines…"

Inspector Bailey didn't speak.

She nodded and walked very quietly

around the edge of the barrier, looking for a way in. She tapped on the boards, very gently, until she found a loose one.

When she pushed it, it swung open.

"Interesting…"

Marlin came through the gap behind her.

The whole place was empty!

"They've gone!"

Inspector Bailey looked at him.

"But I'm telling the truth Inspector," he protested. "They were here!"

"*Who* were here?" said a voice suddenly.

Oliver Grubbler stepped out of the shadows and loomed over Marlin.

"Ah, Mr Grubbler," said Inspector Bailey. "Perhaps you can help us. This young man says he saw a lot of demolition trucks in here a while ago. Where have they gone?"

"Demolition trucks?" laughed Grubbler. "Dear me no, Inspector! The boy is mistaken – those trucks were never here!"

He reached out a beefy hand to ruffle Marlin's hair and Marlin took a step back.

Grubbler smiled.

"You know what boys are like. I expect

he's been watching too many films…"

"But what is that?" continued Inspector Bailey, pointing towards the big black machine. It was still crouched exactly where Marlin had seen it.

"That," said another voice, "is our new attraction!"

A man in a neat suit stepped through the doorway behind them.

"It's wonderful isn't it? The Mayor himself will be opening it tomorrow night. We've sold lots of tickets. I think the whole town will be here!"

And then he gave a small bow.

"I'm Howard H. Snickenbacker by the way."

"I'm Inspector Bailey," replied the Inspector. "Now perhaps you could tell me. What exactly is it?"

Snickenbacker smiled. He took his phone from his pocket, raised it in the air, and pressed a button.

Suddenly the black machine was covered with sparkling lights. Then it began to turn gently, round and round, and music drifted across the square.

"It's a fairground ride of course," said Snickenbacker. "Whatever did you think it was?"

*******

"Don't worry," said Inspector Bailey. She was taking Marlin home in her car.

"I know you weren't lying to me. But it's easy to make mistakes. Sometimes things aren't what we imagine."

Marlin nodded glumly.

The Inspector stopped the car outside his house.

"I'm going to investigate and find out where all those trucks are. You can stop worrying. Stay at home and get some rest."

*******

Marlin lay in bed unable to sleep. The moon shone hard and bright through his window and he stared up at it.

They were out there somewhere…right now the hunters were heading towards the mountain, he knew it.

He could picture them, roaring along empty roads, racing through sleeping towns and villages.

Mile by mile they were closing-in on their prey.

The Dinoteks would be asleep – Protos in his cave with his fossils, Flame under his trees, and the others, all in their special places.

None of them knew about the danger approaching.

Marlin sat up.

He couldn't lie here any longer! He had to do something.

He looked up at the precious letter that Protos had given him, his closest link with the Dinoteks. And as the moon shone in through his window, and onto the wall where the piece of paper was pinned, Marlin saw it.

At the bottom of the paper was a little squiggle that he hadn't spotted before.

He leaned closer. Yes! It was writing – tiny letters – PTO...

Marlin pulled the pins out and grabbed the note off the wall.

PTO...*Please Turn Over!*

Marlin flipped the paper over and found this:

PS. DEAR MARLIN – PLEASE COME AND VISIT US SOON. WE'LL BE WAITING FOR YOU!

DACKY WILL COME AND GET YOU ON THE LONGEST DAY OF THE YEAR (THAT'S THE SUMMER SOLSTICE ACTUALLY). YOU

CAN MEET HIM AT MIDNIGHT IN THE PLACE WHERE THE GIANT SNAKE LIVES – I'M SURE YOU REMEMBER THAT.

LOVE PROTOS.

Yes! Marlin knew exactly where Protos meant. It was the place where they had found the train and escaped from the city.

But, the longest day of the year? When was that? Soon?

Marlin ran downstairs to the kitchen. His mum's calendar was pinned to the wall and all the days were crossed through with a pen, right up to today – and on today's square was written: June 21, Summer Solstice.

*Dacky was coming tonight!*

He looked up at the kitchen clock. It was 11.15pm already.

He had to get to the railway – and he had to be there by midnight!

# Chapter Eight

........

## Dacky
## in the Dark

Marlin waited.
 He had the old leather jacket
on again and his back-pack full of
tools.

He felt good.

There might be trouble to come,
but he wasn't worried – he was going
back to the mountain and when he
got there, he was sure he would know
what to do.

Somehow he would protect the
Dinoteks and everything would be all
right.

He stared up at the sky, peering
towards the north. The moon was

still bright and he looked for a distant flash
of silver – that would be the first sign of
Dacky approaching.

He watched and waited.

*******

Dacky didn't come.

Marlin was in the right place, he was sure
of it. He was standing on a log – the very
one that Steg and Protos had climbed on,
to reach the train. The jagged tooth marks
were still there at one end where Flame had
picked it up.

And further along he could see deep
scuffs in the gravel. That's where Flame had
fallen over, then scrambled to his feet again.

He looked up at the sky.

*Come on… come on Dacky…*

What if the hunters had reached the
mountain already?

What if Dacky had been caught?

Marlin stared into the north and saw
nothing but stars.

And as Marlin stared north, looking

intently into the night sky, Dacky flew out of the east and crashed to the ground.

******

"Are you OK? What happened?!" The creature lifted his head and tried to fold his twisted wings.

"Sorry I'm late boy…had some trouble…"

Marlin ran along to his wing tips and gently pushed, helping the creature to tuck them in.

"Got lost… the flying machine attacked me…"

"The helicopter?!"

Dacky nodded.

"Yes… it chased me…tried to…it was too slow though, not skillful like me…"

The Pterosaur laughed.

"I would have been quicker to get here… but I couldn't find the way…and my batteries are running low…"

"Don't worry!" said Marlin. "I'll fix that!"

He delved into his back-pack – then realised that he didn't have the power charger. Of course – it was still on the mountain with the Dinoteks! He glanced at the Pterosaur.

"Dacky, I… Dacky?!"

But the giant creature was frozen – just a sleeping statue again.

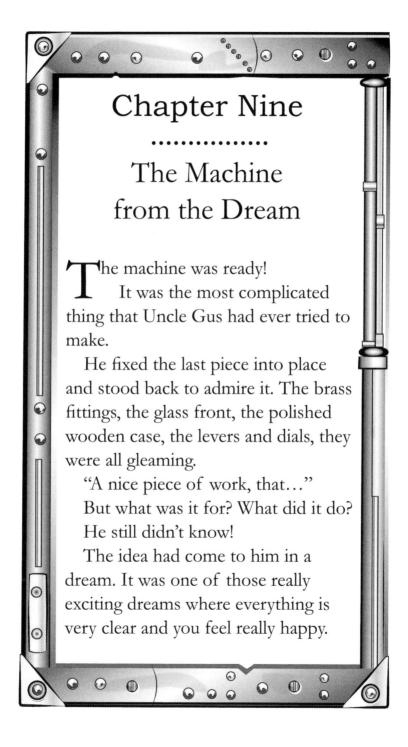

# Chapter Nine

·················

## The Machine
from the Dream

The machine was ready!
It was the most complicated
thing that Uncle Gus had ever tried to
make.

He fixed the last piece into place
and stood back to admire it. The brass
fittings, the glass front, the polished
wooden case, the levers and dials, they
were all gleaming.

"A nice piece of work, that…"

But what was it for? What did it do?
He still didn't know!

The idea had come to him in a
dream. It was one of those really
exciting dreams where everything is
very clear and you feel really happy.

That had been a couple of weeks ago.

Uncle Gus had woken up smiling – the sun was shining in on him and it seemed like it would be a perfect day. He'd jumped out of bed and quickly drawn a picture of the machine in his notebook. Straight away he'd started making it.

And now, tonight, he'd finally finished!

He rubbed his hands together.

"So then… let's see what you do, exactly…"

He wasn't sure… but he had an idea that he should press down one of the brass levers.

### BLEEP! BLEEP! CLUNK!

Yes! It was working!

Now he worked furiously, not thinking …

Quick! Press that button – and turn that knob – no, no, not that one, the other one! That's it – three times to the left…

There was a wooshing sound – and suddenly the room was filled with sparkling lights – fizzing around him like little golden fireworks.

And Uncle Gus was amazed. Because suddenly he began to remember things that he had long forgotten.

He knew exactly what the machine was for and why he had built it.

\*\*\*\*\*\*

Marlin looked miserably at the frozen Pterosaur. Tears pricked at his eyes and he struggled to take out Dacky's battery. He wiped his face angrily with the back of his sleeve.

He must keep a clear head!

The grey cylinder was cold and heavy in his hands.

His earlier brave spirits drained away. He needed Uncle Gus to tell him what to do!

And then suddenly it happened – the most amazing and unexpected thing.

The battery in Marlin's hands began to glow. Lights appeared, fizzing and sparkling like little fireworks.

It was just like before – all those weeks ago when Protos had woken up in the

museum and talked to him!

Marlin didn't understand how it could be happening, or why it was happening, but right now he didn't need to.

He dropped down beside Dacky and pushed the battery back into place.

The Pterosaur's eyes snapped open.

"Well done boy!" he cawed.

The great creature scrambled to his feet and unfurled his wide wings.

"Come on now! Let's hurry!"

76

He took Marlin in his claws and suddenly they were in the air together. Marlin gripped onto his legs and he felt the breeze on his face.

Aaak! Aaaak!

"Let's go! Let's fly to the mountain!"

# Chapter Ten

· · · · · · · · · · · · · · · · ·

## An Inspector in a Hurry

The car raced through the sleeping town, passing unseen along its empty streets. The vehicle swerved, its tyres screeched and the driver leaned forward gripping the steering wheel.

Inspector Bailey was in a hurry.

She was on her way back from the Snickenbacker Scrap Metal Headquarters.

It was a big building on the edge of town – a country house, but not a pretty one. Everything was very neat and square, and in the whole wide area around the house there wasn't a single tree, or bush, or blade of grass.

Everything was concrete.

She had parked her car and climbed out. The place seemed deserted.

Then a figure had appeared, stepping out of the shadows by the front door. It was a security guard, a mean looking woman with hard eyes.

"I'm looking for Mr Snickenbacker and Mr Grubbler," said the Inspector. "Have you seen them?"

"They've gone," the guard glowered. "And before you ask, I'm not saying where."

The guard turned her back and began to walk away.

"Wait a moment," said the Inspector.

She pulled out her police badge.

"I'm a Detective Chief Inspector and I'm investigating a possible crime. You'd better answer my questions…"

The guard had glared at her – but spoke.

"They've gone monster hunting. Dinosaurs. Up in the mountains."

*******

Now the Inspector was racing back through the town, using all her driving skill.

The car skidded, but gripped the road.
She knew there wasn't much time.

Dinosaur hunting – Marlin was right! She
should have listened to him.

Now he was at home in bed (so she
thought) and she wouldn't wake him. He
was safe there.

But there was someone else she needed
to see. Someone who might know where the
Dinoteks were hiding…

# Chapter Eleven

· · · · · · · · · · · · · · · ·

## What Steg Discovered

It was dawn. Steg woke – and felt cross, as usual.

Every morning he did the same thing.

He stood for a moment at the door of his ruined house, sniffed the air, shook his armour plates and then stomped off down the mountain.

He was going on patrol.

He'd been feeling grumpy ever since he'd arrived on the mountain and he wasn't quite sure why. Maybe it was because he'd lost one of his tail lights on the way here. Or maybe he didn't like following Protos all the time.

Or maybe he didn't want to be living on a mountain at all.

Yes, maybe that was it.

The mountain was beautiful, especially in the early morning light. But Steg still missed the Professor and he just wanted to be back at the museum with everything normal again, the way it used to be.

He stomped on.

He knew that Protos was expecting him to come up to the cave this morning – something special was happening apparently – but now Steg decided to ignore that.

"I'm not going. Whatever it is, they can do it without me," he snorted.

He wouldn't go.

Instead he followed the path that led downwards, winding through the trees.

*******

"Can you see Marlin? Is he coming?! Is he coming?!" squeaked Siggy.

"I'm sure he'll be here very soon," nodded Protos.

They were standing by his cave and Protos had laid out all his latest fossil finds.

"I think he'll like this one best…or maybe that one…no, no, this one…"

Comp and Siggy were very excited.

"I hope Dacky doesn't drop him," squeaked Comp.

Siggy nodded.

"Yes, I hope that too."

Little Dragon took off and began buzzing round in circles.

"Don't be silly. Of course Dacky won't drop him," chuckled Flame.

Protos stopped looking at his fossils. He lumbered over to the edge of the clearing and began peering anxiously into the trees.

"Oh dear! Where is Steg? Doesn't he want to be here when Marlin arrives?"

"He's sulking," grunted Flame. "He's always sulking. Shall I go and find him?"

But Protos didn't answer. He was staring intently into the distance.

Suddenly he turned round and he looked worried.

"I think I should go," he said quickly.

"Flame, will you look after everyone here?"

"If that's what you want," grunted Flame.

"Yes it is," said the old Centrosaurus. "Stay together. Stay up here, and wait for Marlin."

And without another word he heaved himself round and set off down the mountain.

The Dinoteks watched him go then turned to look back up into the sky.

None of them noticed what Protos had seen.

There was a road far below, winding across the hills. And a line of tiny black dots had appeared on it, far away, but getting closer.

Something (or some *things*) was driving towards the mountain.

*******

Steg arrived at the bottom of the mountain. The river was in front of him, with a bridge crossing over it.

This was the end of the Dinoteks' territory. Steg had put the sign up here – the one that Marlin had made.

*The Jurassic Mountain – this safe territory belongs to the Dinoteks…*

Steg checked it.

"Good," he snorted.

Then he marched onwards, across the bridge and onto the grassy meadow below. This wasn't Dinotek land any more – but he didn't see why he should have to stay on the mountain all the time.

He liked the meadow.

He liked the way the grass moved in waves every time the wind blew. And he liked the fresh smell of the flowers. And the buzzing sound of the grass-hoppers all around him and…suddenly Steg stopped walking.

He really liked the meadow…

And maybe that's why it happened.

Maybe that's why the same wild magic that had worked on Marlin now worked on Steg too.

He suddenly realised how wonderful this

place was – and how glad it made him feel.

He stood there looking around him in the bright morning sun and it was as if he was seeing it all for the very first time!

He stood there, just enjoying it – and afterwards he couldn't say whether he stood in that place for a few seconds, or minutes or even hours – but when he finally shook his head and looked about again, he discovered that something inside him had changed.

"I've been very silly!" he told himself. "Very, very silly. All these days I've been grumpy – but what a waste of good days!"

And suddenly he knew that he wanted one thing, more than any other – he wanted to go back to his friends and have fun with them. He wanted to jump in the river with Flame and collect fossils with Protos. He wanted to cheer as Dacky and Little Dragon flew over the mountain. And he wanted to play hide and seek with Siggy and Comp and let them run round him and jump over his tail.

He turned to go back. And that's when

he saw the black trucks racing towards him across the hillside.

*******

Steg stared at the trucks, amazed. There were so many of them. So many!

They rolled on like a black wave, spreading out to surround him, and he stood there unable even to move…

"Steg! Quick! Run!" ordered a voice.

The words cut through his panic and Steg turned to see Protos lumbering across the meadow towards him.

"Run!" called Protos again – and that was all that Steg needed.

He moved at last. He powered forwards, racing up the hillside towards his friend, proving that large creatures can be quick as well as strong.

"That's it!" urged Protos. "Well done Steg! Keep going!"

Steg reached him.

"Thank you! Thank you for coming!" he

panted.

"But don't stop now!" ordered Protos. "Get back up the mountain!"

"OK! Let's go!"

Steg led the way.

The bridge wasn't close – but now he was going faster than he ever knew he could.

"Follow me! Follow me!" Steg shouted as he raced onwards.

But Protos wasn't following.

# Chapter Twelve

· · · · · · · · · · · · · · · · ·

## Protos Alone

Protos turned to face the hunters. He was too slow and he knew it. One of his back legs never did work very well.

There was no point running, not for him.

But he could hold the hunters back long enough for Steg to escape.

He stepped forward and chose the best place to stand.

*******

Protos imagined himself back in the Cretaceous era and he pictured himself not standing there alone, but with a herd of Centrosauruses all around him.

That made him feel braver.

He knew a nice story about Centrosauruses and he had often practised it, so that one day he might tell it to visitors to the museum.

When Centrosauruses were attacked they would stand side by side, lining up their shields in a great circle, with their young sheltering behind them. Their sharp horns faced outwards like a bank of spears. What a sight! Even the mighty T-Rex would think twice about tackling them!

That's what Protos was thinking about as the first truck hit him.

He staggered backwards and turned his head, tilting the truck away. It skidded and rolled away into the grass. In the cab, the

driver glared at him – but he wasn't injured.

"Remember the Second Golden Rule," thought Protos. "Never hurt anybody…"

He heaved himself back to face the next truck.

It rammed him and he butted it away too.

He snorted and pawed at the ground.

Steg must be nearly at the bridge by now.

And then the third truck struck, much harder and faster.

He shoved it away again, crumpling its bonnet, and he somehow stayed on his feet.

But at the same moment there was a terrible CRACK – it was a sharp, painful sound that echoed across the mountain – and Protos's horn shattered, falling in pieces around him.

He turned to face the next attack but he had lost his main defence.

His legs felt wobbly now, but he stood square and still blocked the way.

The fourth vehicle was a huge black digger. It roared forwards.

And while that was happening nobody noticed a shadow racing across the meadow.

A great winged creature soared overhead.

The black digger stopped right in front of Protos.

A figure climbed out. A large man, in a suit.

Grubbler.

"So, you like fighting do you?"

"Not very much," Protos said. "I prefer collecting fossils."

Grubbler glared at him.

"Well too bad! Because when you get back to the museum it's fighting you'll be doing! We've got a nice fighting machine all lined up for you!"

"I could give you a guided tour of the museum instead," said Protos. "It's really very interesting…"

"I'm the museum manager!" roared Grubbler. "I don't need a guided tour!"

"But have you seen the collection of rare musical instruments? There's a lovely flute made by…"

"Enough!" roared Grubbler.

And he raised his hand.

The digger revved its engine, smoke billowed around it, and its roar echoed across the mountain.

Its jaws lifted, snapping. The sound of the roar grew louder and louder and shook the air.

But it wasn't coming from the digger.

It was the roar of a T-Rex.

*******

Flame crashed onto the grass in front of the digger and sunk his teeth into it. The driver jumped out, terrified, as the T-Rex stamped down onto the cabin.

Grubbler took one look at Flame and ran.

**P**rotos collapsed. Steg came racing across the grass.

"Is he OK? Flame! Did you save him?!"

Dacky swooped down and Marlin scrambled onto the ground beside Protos.

The old creature's armour was dented and he looked smaller without his horn. His eyes were closed.

"Protos! Can you hear me?" Marlin said, pressing his face close.

But Protos didn't answer and Steg looked down horrified.

"It's my fault!" he sobbed.

But Marlin shook his head, determined.

"Don't cry," he said. "Don't worry Steg. I can help him. I just need the tools…"

First he would use the Golden Power Charger to give Protos energy, then he would clean him up, then – but even as he was thinking this he heard the rattle and squeak of big machines moving. He looked up and saw all the trucks now surrounding them – dozens of them, a great army.

Too many for even Flame to fight.

And now Grubbler had returned too.

He clambered up onto the wreck of the first digger and puffed out his chest.

"Time to give up! All of you!" he ordered.

"No," said a second voice. "It's time for *you* to give up!"

Grubbler turned

"Eh?"

Inspector Bailey was standing right behind him.

# Chapter Thirteen

••••••••••••••••

## What Went Wrong and how it Came Right Again

"You can't stop me!" protested Grubbler. "These dinosaurs belong to the museum. *My* museum!"

"But it's not your museum," said Bailey. "You're only the manager – in fact you're not even that."

"I am …what…what do you mean?"

The Inspector pointed towards her car.

"The real manager is back – and his name is Professor Cogwell!"

The car door opened and an old

man climbed out.

Marlin gasped.

It was Uncle Gus.

*******

"Well done lad!" beamed Uncle Gus, waving to Marlin. "And you are in big trouble!" he said, pointing at Grubbler.

Siggy ran forwards.

"Professor! Professor! You've gone old!"

"Yes, I'm sorry about that Siggy. I'm afraid I lost my memory for a bit – but don't worry, I'm back now."

He clapped his hands.

"It's so good to see you all! Flame, you're looking wonderful – and Dacky! I didn't know you could actually fly!"

"Uncle Gus! I don't understand…" exclaimed Marlin.

"It was that machine, lad! The one I've been building. Last night I turned it on – and all these golden sparks came out – and I suddenly remembered everything! I remembered that years ago I made a machine just like it – it's what first brought the Dinoteks to life. Only one day my young assistant tampered with it…"

He glowered at Grubbler.

"I…I didn't mean to," stuttered Grubbler, looking suddenly small. "I didn't know it would go wrong…"

"Well it did," said Inspector Bailey. "And it made the poor Professor forget everything."

"No, not quite everything," said Uncle Gus. "I remembered a little bit about Protos. And I knew the Dinoteks were special… I just didn't remember that it was me who made them."

"So that's why the Professor disappeared!" exclaimed Marlin. "That's why the Dinoteks fell asleep!"

"Yes – until you woke them up again! What a brilliant lad you are. In fact you're all brilliant!"

"But Professor!" exclaimed Steg. "What about Protos?"

"Foolish me!" said Uncle Gus. "Enough talking!"

He hurried across to kneel beside Protos.

"Hello old friend," he said gently. "Are you hurt?"

And Protos's eyes slowly opened.

"Ah Professor, I knew you'd come back. Everyone is safe. But I'm rather worried about the museum – I'm afraid they've made a terrible mess of it…"

"Don't worry about that, we'll soon have it fixed. We'll soon have everything fixed…"

And Professor Arthur Augustus Cogwell – who is sometimes also known as Uncle Gus – set to work repairing Protos, the oldest and bravest of the Dinoteks.

And as he worked, fixing wires back into place and tightening loose parts, he had help from Marlin Maxton – who, in the future (and there were many adventures after this) would sometimes also be known as Professor Cogwell's Nephew.

# Chapter Fourteen

## The Return of the Dinosaurs

Inspector Bailey made the truck drivers clear up all the mess – the smashed metal, glass and plastic from the damaged vehicles.

"I don't want to see a single scrap left behind!" she ordered.

She made Grubbler help too – but he was still protesting.

He hurried after her, flapping his hands and whispering urgently.

"You can't let these dinosaurs go free," he hissed. "What if they're dangerous?!"

"The only dangerous thing around here is you," snapped the Inspector. "Get on with the cleaning up!"

And then her phone rang.

"Yes? Hello? Ah, Mr Mayor – I've got some very interesting things to tell you…"

*******

And you might think that this is the end of the story – and it nearly is, but not quite.

Because there was one last battle to fight, and Flame had to do something amazing that no T-Rex had ever done before.

Inspector Bailey  finished talking to the Mayor and turned off her phone.

"Well," she sighed. "We have an unexpected problem. It seems that Snickenbacker has turned on his fighting machine and now it's running wild breaking things. Nobody can stop it."

Flame stepped forward.

"We can."

*******

The last time Flame had run back to the city, carrying Marlin in the night, it had taken him four hours. But this time he did it differently – and he did it quicker.

First, he wasn't just carrying Marlin, this time he was carrying Inspector Bailey too.

The detective squeezed in next to Marlin in the high seat and had the most amazing ride of her life. She'd thought police cars were exciting – but this was a hundred times better!

The second thing that Flame did differently is that he didn't run all the way.

No, he took a short cut across the hills and headed towards the railway line. And then he did the most impressive thing you can imagine.

Coming along in the distance, very fast, was the Intercity Express. It was racing towards the city at incredible speed. Flame sprinted forwards to meet it.

"He can't be!" exclaimed Bailey. "It's not possible!"

But it was.

Flame leapt into the air as the train rushed passed – and he timed his jump perfectly.

He landed on top.

In the entire history of this planet no T-Rex has ever done anything like ride on a skateboard. But that day Flame came pretty close.

*******

Dacky reached the city first, swooping out of the sky towards the museum.

He could see the horrible black machine below, snapping its claws and lashing out at the buildings around it.

People were running, trying to get to safety.

And he saw a young girl fall over as the machine came edging towards her.

Dacky dived.

He snatched up the girl and carried her to safety.

Then he went back – again and again – pulling people out of the way of the machine.

*******

Flame arrived next .
He stopped at the edge of the grass square, and told Marlin and Inspector Bailey to climb down.

"This could be dangerous…"

"Flame! Be careful!" exclaimed Marlin.

"Yes," said Bailey. "Don't take any risks!"

But Flame was already moving.

He advanced across the square and stood in front of the giant machine.

And then he saw the man, cowering on the ground beside it.

"Help! Save me!"

It was the Mayor!

Flame dashed forwards to rescue him.

The machine started to follow but Flame fooled it, dodging and weaving out of the way.

The machine spun round and clawed after him as he ran.

*******

The other Dinoteks arrived soon after, riding on the trucks.

Steg rushed forwards to let people shelter

under his armour plates and the Troodons scampered this way and that, as if trying to confuse the big machine.

Then Protos arrived with Uncle Gus.

The old creature was still a bit wobbly, but he looked much better.

Uncle Gus had even fixed him up with a new horn – it was made out of an old tree branch, and still had a few leaves growing on it – but it looked good.

Protos went to stand in front of the giant machine.

"I think you forgot the Three Golden Rules," he said.

The machine turned towards him, jaws snapping, but Protos stepped quickly in. He lowered his horn…and pressed the *off* switch.

"Never hurt anyone."

The machine fell silent.

# Chapter Fifteen

. . . . . . . . . . . . . . . .

## The End of
## one Adventure
## (and Ready for the Next)

And that's how the Dinoteks came back to the city – not as monsters, but as heroes.

For a few days after that there was lots of celebrating, and lots of fuss, but then things got back to normal – almost.

When Marlin got home he told his mum and dad everything – and this time they actually listened.

"Dinosaurs? Really? But why didn't you tell us before?!"

In a few weeks the mess was cleared up and the museum opened again –

but this time it had a very nice manager, called Professor Cogwell, who liked visitors, and never handed out worksheets to children.

And when he wasn't at the museum he could usually be found in his workshop, inventing new things or just chatting with his favourite nephew and drinking tea. Or hot chocolate. Or both.

Howard H. Snickenbacker sold his scrap metal company and left the city in a hurry. Nobody knows where he went. And nobody cares.

And Grubbler hid himself away at home, which was the best place for him.

The Dinoteks Show opened too – and each day when visitors arrived at the door they were met by a very knowledgeable and interesting Centrosaurus who could answer all their questions about dinosaurs before taking them on a wonderful tour around a secret, forgotten room.

Only that room wasn't secret or forgotten any more. It was the most important room in the museum – the room where the

Dinoteks lived.

And the Dinoteks were very happy.

Especially Steg. Because no matter what happened, whether it was raining outside or sunny, whether it was a holiday or a day for work, Steg was always cheerful.

He was famous for it.

And if anyone ever asked him why, he would just laugh.

"Being grumpy is the waste of a lovely day."

**The End...
for now**

# *The Secret Dinosaur #4*
## A new adventure

It's the end of one adventure - and the start of another!
Marlin, Flame, Protos and the others are back in Book 4.

In this exciting adventure Marlin makes a fantastic new discovery about the Dinoteks… but trouble is not far behind.

**Find out more at www.dinoteks.com**

*The Secret Dinosaur books are available online or you can order them from your local bookshop.*

# The Dinosaur Book Room

Do you remember how the Dinoteks escaped through a secret passage? The entance to the tunnel was in a wonderful room packed full of dinosaur books. Well, would you like a quick look inside? There's just time before we go, and perhaps you'll find some new dinosaur facts or long forgotten stories. Come on in...

Are you an **expert?** Try this quiz!

Well, this is lucky for you, Protos has prepared a special dinsoaur quiz! He says it will be very educational and actually quite good fun too.

Hmm. He's has even included a few jokes (so please remember to laugh...)

### 1. Pterosaurs probably ate:

(a) Fish, insects and small land animals

(b) Vegetation

(c) Anything they could find in the fridge

### 2. Tyrannosaurus Rex means:

(a) Deadly giant carnivore

(b) King of the tyrant lizards

(c) I'm so big I need two names

## 3. What did Stegosaurs use their back plates for?

(a) A display to impress enemies

(b) Controlling body temperature

(c) Perhaps both (a) and (b)

(b) For wind-surfing across lakes

## 4. When did Centrosaurines roam the earth?

(a) In the Permian era

(b) In the Ice Age

(c) In the Cretaceous era

(b) Whenever they got lost

## 5. What sort of dinosaurs are Troodons?

(a) Arthropods

(b) Therapods

(c) Cute but a bit naughty

Easy? You'll be able to check all your answers in the next few pages...

# A stout and bulky Ceratopsian

Diet: herbivore
Typical food: tough vegetation
When it lived: late Cretaceous
Length: up to 6m     Height: up to 2m
Weight: up to 1000kg
Where found: Canada
Pronounced: Cen-TROH-sore-us
Name means: sharp pointed lizard

The
Centrosaurus
Encylopedia
_____
Third Edition

Centrosaurus was a bulky, four-legged dinosaur with an impressive frill over its head and neck.
This may have been a defensive shield or a display to frighten enemies and attract mates.
It may also have helped the creature regulate its body temperature - either warming itself, perhaps by facing toward the sun early in the morning, or cooling itself on hot days by fanning the

air, much as elephants do today.

At first glance Centrosaurus looks quite similar to its famous cousin, the Triceratops - and both are members of the Ceratopsian family of dinosaurs.

But notice the big difference: Centrosaurus has only one horn, not three. Centrosaurus was also rather smaller than Triceratops.

However, by today's reckoning it was still a very large animal - and with that forward-facing horn as its main weapon it would have been able to stand and fight, if it had to.

It is easy enough to imagine large herds of Centrosaurines grouping together to repel an attack by the large predators such as Tyrannosaurs that hunted in the late Cretaceous.

# Giants of the skies

Scientific name: Pteranodon
Typical food: fish
When it lived: late Cretaceous
Wingspan: 7m to 9m
Where found: North America
Pronounced: Teh-RAN-no-DON
Name means: Wings and no teeth

Pteranodon was not a dinosaur, but a flying reptile. It was among the largest of its kind and would have been a superb flier. In fact the shape of its wings suggests that it had a very efficient flying technique. It would have used rising air currents to travel incredible distances without wasting energy - riding high into the sky then gliding for miles, hunting for food.

Many different species of Pteranodon have been found, with different shapes and sizes of head crest.

# A herbivore with impressive defences

Scientific name: Stegosaurus
Typical food: low growing vegetation
When it lived: late Jurassic
Length: up to 9m    Height: up to 4m
Where found: Europe, North America
Pronounced: STEG-oh-SORE-us
Name means: roof lizard

Stegosaurus is one of the most spectacular looking dinosaurs. Fossil remains that have been discovered show that in real life this would have been an impressive and formidable creature.

Its most notable feature is the double-row of armoured plates running right along its back. These plates make Stegosaurus look taller and bulkier, almost giving it the appearance of a living castle. But what were those rows of plates really for?

A clue has been found in the form of tiny grooves running across the surface of some

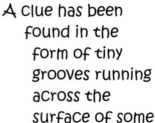

particularly well preserved fossil plates.
Some scientists think these grooves show
where blood vesels may have run.
If so, then the creature may have pumped

blood across the plates, perhaps to regulate
its temperature or to create a bright display
to warn off its enemies.
This was not its only defence - like modern
animals that use bright colours as a warning
(such as wasps), Stegosaurus could also
inflict painful injuries. The massive spikes on
its tail would have been dangerous for any
creature foolish enough to venture within
its range.

# Clever little hunters

Scientific name: Troodon
Typical food: small creatures
When it lived: late Cretaceous
Length: up to 2.4m
Where found: North America
Pronounced: TROO-a-DON
Name means: wounding tooth

Troodons were among the last of the dinosaurs, living during the late Cretaceous era and they were part of the same Therapod group as birds - meaning that they are closely related to creatures still alive today.

It is very probable that Troodons had feathers or down, not for flying but for added protection against the cold and also for display.

Troodons would have been too small to tackle larger dinosaurs as they were no

bigger than an adult human is today.
But they had sharp claws and teeth. They
would have been nimble and clever hunters,
adept at catching the many small creatures
that teemed across the Cretaceous
landscape, such as lizards, snakes, mammals
and birds.

Troodons had large eyes and big brains for
their body size, suggesting that they were
among the cleverest of dinosaurs. Their
eyes would have equipped them well for
hunting at dusk and their feathery down
would have allowed them to remain active
in cooler night temperatures. Unlike T-Rex
they would also have used their long clawed
hands for catching prey.

# Glimpse into a vanished world

Scientific name: Meganeura
Typical food: insects
When it lived: late Carboniferous
Length: up to 70cm
Where found: Europe
Pronounced: MEG-ah-NYER-ah

In the lush, tropical forests of the Carboniferous, long before the dinosaurs evolved, a gigantic, early dragonfly darted above the water hunting for insects. Meganeura had a wingspan reaching up to 70cm, making it a true colossus compared to today's dragonflies.

But the shape of its body, so beautifully streamlined, is very similar to modern species, suggesting that it probably hunted in a similar way.

With skillful, darting flight and rapid changes of direction it would chase and catch other insects in mid-air.

Watch any modern dragonfly, hunting exactly like this on a summer's day, and you are getting a glimpse back into an age long vanished - it's a wonderful sight.

# The most famous predator of them all

Scientific name: Tyrannosaurus Rex
Typical food: all prey species
When it lived: late Cretaceous
Length: up to 12m
Weight: up to 5 tonnes
Where found: North America
Pronounced: Tie-RAN-o-SOR-us REX
Name means: King of the Tyrant Lizards

Tyrannosaurus Rex will probably always be the most famous land predator, even though the fossil remains of bigger hunters have been discovered.

T-Rex may have been slightly smaller than some of these other predators (such as Giganotosaurus and some types of Spinosaur) but it still holds the record for the strongest jaws and the most powerful bite.

The strength of its bite can be estimated from the shape of its skull and the thickness of its teeth - both were well suited to pulling apart tough armoured skin and crunching bones.

T-Rex also has a relatively short body and powerful neck which would have added to its strength. This would have made it a tough opponent to face, whether you were its prey or another carnivore competing with it for territory.

T-Rex had other advantages too: large eyes and an accute sense of smell would have made it hard to hide from, even if you kept very still.

And one final thought. New Tyrannosaurus remains are still being discovered - so it may be that T-Rex will regain its crown as the largest land predator ever. Somewhere out there, still buried in rock, could be a fossil T-Rex that makes all the others look small...

The answers to the quiz are:
1. (a) 2. (b) 3. (c) 4. (c) 5. (b)

# Come back soon!

There are so many good books to read and you've only just begun...